Quantum Lace

~ BOOK TWO ~

Quantum Lace

Book Two

Dedicated to all the lives that were lost and
touched as a result of the
Lancastria tragedy.

...Lest we forget...

Requests for permission to reproduce parts of this
work should be addressed to the author.
Contact information can be found here:

www.QuantumLace.com

If you would like to invite the author to speak at an
event for your organization, please contact
Leigh (Bella) St John via the website.

The contents of this book are the intellectual property
of the author, who deserves to be compensated for the
time and energy invested in this work.

Copyright © 2017 Leigh St John aka Bella St John

*Thank you and I hope you
enjoy the book...*

Prologue

While you can read this as a stand-alone short story, it is preferable if you first read Book One where you not only learn how Bridgit came to be in the predicament in which she finds herself at the beginning of this book, but also the background information and science behind how she is able to time travel – and why she chooses to do so.

Links to Book One on Amazon:
US Customers:
http://bit.ly/quantumlace
UK Customers:
http://bit.ly/quantumlace-uk

Introduction

The story of time-travel you are about to read, while a work of fiction, is largely based on real science, real people and real events. Where fact leaves off and fiction begins is for you to decide.

Do a search on just about anything in this book and make up your own mind what is 'real'…

Table of Contents

Prologue 3

Introduction 4

Chapter One …and then…................... 6

Chapter Two – Salvation… 12

Chapter Three – Journey 'Home' 31

Chapter Four – "This Never Happened" 49

Chapter Five – Plymouth 55

Chapter Six – Hastings 45 Years Later…
.... 66

Chapter Seven – Revelation 90

Chapter Eight – What is 'Now'? 102

…and then…...................................... 121

Acknowledgements 124

Thank you… 128

About the Author 130

Chapter One ...and then...

Bridgit awoke to find herself clinging to a life preserver, her fingers latched together with such force, at first she was unable to separate them.

As she looked around through squinted, stinging eyes, Bridgit saw the extent of the devastation – and now that she had unlocked her fingers, her grasp was continually slipping from the floatation device due to the slimy, thick layer of oil that carpeted the sea and her body alike.

Scattered like toothpicks across the water were dead bodies, fragments of wood, severed limbs, chairs, military packs... Occasionally she would see among the countless others a figure floating that appeared at first glance to be deceased, only to realize there was life remaining within when a gaze of white eyeballs and penetrating pupils through the black oil-covered flesh revealed a soul clinging to hope.

Not far away, a collection of soldiers was standing on what looked like a beached whale the size of a small city, slowly sinking into the water – this was the upended hull of what she would later learn was His Majesty's Troopship (HMT) Lancastria, and Bridgit had found herself in the English Channel off the coast of St Nazaire on June 17th, 1940 in the worst maritime disaster in British history.

"Oh, God... Oh, dear God!" Bridgit's internal disbelieving cry as she continued to struggle with her grasp on the precious life preserver echoed the chorus of "God help me!" and "God save me, I can't swim!" she heard from those adrift. As Bridgit's mind raced, she searched for any semblance of logic or rationality to help calm herself and make sense of her situation; and wondered at that moment what atheists call out in times of trouble..?

Further calming and composing herself, little by little, Bridgit surveyed the situation.

Among the obvious pandemonium and chaos, there was also a bizarre sense of calm and unruffled composure among the masses.

The soldiers standing on the hull were singing as though revelling in a village pub. The song was unfamiliar to Bridgit, but the words rang true of the country she loved. "There'll always be an England while there's a country lane, wherever there's a cottage small beside a field of grain." Another group, carousing and singing "roll out the barrel" with gusto.

Having now found a firm hold on her flotation device, Bridgit continued to take in what, in every possible, conceivable way was an alien scene that bore no resemblance to anything Bridgit knew and loved of the world she had left only hours ago – or was it only minutes..?

A smartly dressed officer standing on the sinking keel smoked a cigarette as evenly and steadily as though he were home in front of the fireplace with a brandy in the other hand.

Making his way slowly past her toward the shore, a man smiled bright white teeth at Bridgit through his oil-blackened face and said in a thick Yorkshire accent, "nice day for a swim!" and continued on by.

"This has to be a dream," Bridgit said aloud.

"If only it were, miss," a male voice from behind her replied.

Bridgit spun around and in the process lost her grip on the oil-covered, slippery life preserver. She felt herself go below the water and inadvertently took a gulp of salty oil as she went under...

Suddenly the noises from above were muted as she sank below the surface. Even her coughing and spluttering made no sound under the water, but the more she coughed, the faster and deeper she sank...

At first Bridgit fought with every intensity to ascend and emerge from the murky subaquatic blanket that seemed to be pulling her every downward, until she finally stopped struggling...

"Remember the tuning forks... You don't want to be feeling anxious when you do this or you'll find yourself in a war zone somewhere in time..." Markus' words of caution rang clear and loud in Bridgit's mind, repeating ever softer and softer, as she felt her life-force drift away and passed into unconsciousness.

Chapter Two - Salvation...

"No you don't!" Bridgit heard the words as though they were muffled through a closed door.

She felt her chest and back being simultaneously compressed as she took a gasp of air...

"That's better, that's it. Just breathe," said a man as she felt him hold her above the water-line.

Bridgit went to open her eyes, but they felt forced shut with the thick coating of oil over her face. Slowly she was able to squint through the goop to see the concerned eyes of a man staring at her.

"Are you ok?" he asked in a quiet and calming tone.

Barely able to breathe let alone speak, Bridgit nodded her accord to the man.

"I wonder what Dixon will say when she sees me in this state?" Bridgit mused to herself. "Or *will* she see me?"

Bridgit felt the rawness of her throat as she attempted to swallow back the tears that were forcing their way to the surface. The nausea was overwhelming but Bridgit was determined to keep the contents of her stomach in place. She pursed her lips and started taking long, slow, deep breaths in and out...

"That's right, m'lady. Long, slow breaths." In her mind, Bridgit saw Dixon standing over her as she lay on the stable-block floor.

"I feel sick, Dixon," Bridgit mumbled before going back to slow breath in, slow breath out.

"He was right behind me... I don't understand..." Bridgit's eyes darted back and forth, recalling every minute detail of the last two hours with George Henry Wadsworth. The colour of the sky, the way the clouds were formed, the smell of horse and leather, the feeling of excitement then alarm then unbridled freedom as she cleared hedge after hedge... but no matter how she searched her thoughts, Bridgit could not recall any memory that reconciled with the news that her fiancé was dead.

Something brushed against Bridgit's body and brought her awareness back to her oil-covered reality, just as she was swiftly yanked back under the water.

She felt something tugging at her leg and furiously kicked to remove it. Bridgit felt her foot connect time and again with something solid, but still it held fast to her. A scuffle erupted beside her under the water, then just as suddenly as it had appeared, she felt whatever was holding her leg release its grasp and someone help her back up to the surface.

Seconds later the man she had previously encountered surfaced. He looked at her and demanded, "stay right there – just stay afloat and stay right there. If anyone else grabs you, kick for dear life. Do you understand?" he yelled. Bridgit nodded as he then swam away.

What seemed like an eternity later, the man reappeared with a large plank floating under his arms.

"Hold on to this," he barked the order at Bridgit. "I will find you a way to get to shore. Just stay here and stay afloat!" With that, he was again gone.

As alone as Bridgit felt when her father had passed away was nothing compared to how alone she felt floating in this sea of dead and dying.

In the distance, Bridgit heard a low-pitched rumble and saw overhead what she would later learn was a British plane circle the continually sinking Lancastria.

In Bridgit's time of 1895, planes were a thing of imagination, usually only found within the drawings of Da Vinci, but now she was in the middle of a global conflict where planes were not only a reality, they made a huge difference to the end result of the war.

British aviator, Norman Hancock brought his Hurricane in over the Lancastria wreckage and threw his own life jacket down to the cheering survivors below before veering off and returning to base to refuel.

Moments later, Bridgit heard another low roar that became lower and lower... until it was accompanied by a rapid and loud 'tk, tk, tk.'

German fighters, seeing an easy target, menaced the survivors by strafing the water with bullets. The air was filled with whistling and whirring sounds – every one of them lethal.

The sound was deafening but once they had passed, Bridgit watched as the Lancastria, only twenty-or-so minutes after initially being hit, succumbed and went under the murky water, down to the depths, quietly and gracefully, sucking hundreds more to their death.

After the Dunkirk evacuation, only a few days earlier, Winston Churchill had assured the people of Britain that "the British Expeditionary Force has been completely and successfully evacuated from France".

Unfortunately, as is often done in times of war, the facts became 'massaged' and that piece of misinformation belied the approximate 150,000 troops still-remaining in now-occupied France.

Not knowing what else to do but to follow the instructions given by her new 'friend', Bridgit stayed put, clutching her plank; mesmerised by the human drama playing out before her.

At one point, she saw an already-overcrowded life-boat whose passengers included a young boy and his dog, making their way to land. Bridgit thought it strange that one vessel would be carrying soldiers, men, women and children alike.

She watched as two young soldiers, who would not have been more than twenty, remained afloat by holding hands across a raft of dead bodies... Only to witness them moments later nod to each other as one man shot his friend and then himself in quick succession.

Bridgit's choices were but two - hold on and hope that her friend would return with salvation, or let go and sink...

~~~~~

"Do you come here often?" asked a cheeky male voice from behind.

Bridgit turned around to see the smiling face of the man who had now saved her more than once.

"I don't think we have been introduced," he said. "My name is Jack Dempsey." As he adjusted himself on his floatation plank Jack extended his right hand toward Bridgit with a grin.

"Lady Bridgit Darnell," she replied with a shy smile as she reached her hand out to touch his.

"Well, well... 'Lady' Bridgit... Let's see what we can do to get your ladyship back to dry land, shall we?" Jack smiled at Bridgit in a way that she instinctively trusted him, although when he said, "We are going to slowly make our way to that boat over there - do you see it?" pointing in the direction of what appeared to be a fishing boat a million miles away, she replied hesitantly, "can't we just swim for shore?"

Rolling his eyes and letting out a laugh, Jack calmly and slowly, as though educating a child, said, "shore is about five or six miles that way", pointing in the direction of St Nazaire, "while that fishing boat is about two miles that way," pointing toward the small speck of a boat in the distance.

"You are more than welcome to swim for shore, but I recommend the boat," he smiled.

Not sure she liked either option, Bridgit felt paralyzed, frozen, unable to move nor even think...

...and then, as though she could muster no more strength to make sense of this hell in which she had found herself, tears began to sting her eyes and sobbing from the depths of her soul overtook her.

So much had happened in such a short time. Only a few weeks ago when her father died, Bridgit thought then that she had lost everything – but finding herself in this hell-hole, she suddenly realised absolutely everything was now truly gone.

Jack made his way close enough to Bridgit to keep her afloat and do his best to simply hold her as she wept. Even the inappropriate proximity of this man was lost on Bridgit. The one and only thing she knew right now was... Actually, there was nothing, not one thing she knew right now... She felt lost and hollow and without hope... and very, very alone.

Eventually, the flood of emotion began to abate and as Bridgit sniffled, Jack peeled the oil-clogged hair from in front of her face. "Ready?" he asked with a cajoling smile.

"Ready," replied Bridgit, taking a deep breath. "Lead on, Macduff," Bridgit replied in an attempt to regain her self-control and poise.

What was originally a flotilla of nineteen vessels sent for the evacuation of the remaining BEF troops was now growing as French fishing vessels began coming to the rescue...

"Did you know that is a misquotation?" asked Bridgit out of the blue as they slowly progressed, her words halting and breathless but with the sound of determination to keep going, keep pressing on.

Jack coughed out a laugh as he looked at Bridgit but kept on kicking slowly toward the boat. "You're quite something, you know. OK, I'll bite. What is a misquotation?"

Bridgit took some time before she could muster the strength to reply. "Lead on, Macduff," she said. "It's actually, "Lay on, Macduff"," she took a deep breath, "from Macbeth."

"I'll be sure to remember that," said Jack through a moderately contained chuckle.

The two did not exchange another word until after they were hauled onto the deck of a French fishing boat.

With a fluency that caught Bridgit off-guard, Jack asked in French for a blanket for Bridgit and somewhere for her to sit.

The deck of the trawler was already filled with black, oil-covered beings but a place was made for Bridgit and soon a blanket was forthcoming.

Jack bent down and wrapped it tightly around her shoulders. "Are you ok?" he asked, not sure what he would be able to do about it if she said no.

Bridgit merely nodded as she began to take in her surroundings.

While normally she would have been appalled at the naked and half naked oil-covered men scattered about the deck, she merely looked at the humanity of the situation, absorbing and doing her best to comprehend.

She saw a woman with a young child and noted the length of the woman's skirt that made her legs visible all the way up to her calves – and realized with muted horror that Bridgit also wore such a revealing garment – but figuring she had more important things about which to worry at present...

The sun was setting as Bridgit became aware of the aroma of something almost sickly sweet.

"Here," said Jack as he handed her a mug of hot liquid. "Take some of this into you – slowly!"

Had this been a British boat, the mug would most likely have contained hot, sweet tea. The French, however, were more partial to wine and Bridgit wasn't sure at first what to make of the mug of hot sweetened wine. Not heeding the 'slowly' suggestion, Bridgit took a few mouthfuls. The urge to vomit engulfed her as she only just made it to the side of the boat before releasing a mixture of sweet wine, salt water and oil from her stomach.

Helping her back to her seat on the edge of a wooden crate, Jack said evenly, "better out than in," and smiled.

It was at that moment Bridgit noticed her companion in a way she had not done before.

He stood reasonably tall at just a little under six feet and she guessed him to be around her age – she was thirty-one; at least she had been when she left home last night...

While his facial features were hidden beneath the oil, Bridgit found herself staring at his shirtless, muscular torso as though admiring a statue in a gallery or museum.

He was wearing what appeared to be a watch on his wrist, held fast with a black leather band. Around his neck suspended from what looked like string were one green octagonal shaped disc, and a red round disc. His trousers were torn and when Bridgit noticed he was only wearing one sock and no shoes, she giggled. She wasn't sure why, but somehow it appealed to her warped sense of humour at that moment.

"I'm not sure what's funny, but it's good to hear you laugh," said Jack. Bridgit merely smiled back at him and clutched her blanket even tighter around her shoulders as she realized he had been watching her staring at him.

The fishing boat approached a large vessel. In the twilight, Bridgit saw huge markings on the side of the ship – 'H44'. They were about to be transferred to the destroyer, "Highlander" for their journey back to England.

Chapter Three – Journey 'Home'

Soon after dawn on June 18th, a convoy of now ten ships with an estimated 23,000 souls aboard, began the journey to Plymouth.

The atmosphere aboard the Highlander was sombre. Few people even moved – fewer spoke.

Bridgit was able to learn from the scarce conversations she did hear that the Lancastria, the ship she had watched sink, was carrying around 9,000 people when she was hit.

"I heard them stop counting around 6,000," said one, "and a good half as many again still got on board after that," said another.

What they would not know at the time was that less than 2,500 people would survive the sinking, leaving an estimated 5,000 to almost 7,000 who perished.

Bridgit saw Jack standing beside the railing, talking to two other men. Despite the subdued tone onboard, the three men appeared to be quite jovial.

When the others moved on, Bridgit approached. "I haven't said thank you," her voice hoarse and she coughed a little in an attempt to clear her throat but all that did was make it sorer.

"No need for thanks as long as you are all right," Jack replied with his now characteristic smile.

The two looked out across the water for several minutes before Bridgit broke the silence.

"Where is 'home' for you," she asked.

"Torquay," Jack replied. "My mother moved there with me when she and my father separated."

"Oh, I'm so sorry," said Bridgit, not sure what to make of this information nor how to react.

Considering they still had many hours before reaching land, Jack decided he may as well continue. "My twin brother

Martin went to Île de Sein with my father and, having been born in France but not wanting to live there again, my mother decided to stay in England and moved the two of us to Torquay where she at least had friends."

Jack stared out at the English Channel for some time before continuing.

"I was only nine but I remember it like it was yesterday," he thought aloud. Then with a slight shake of his head as though just realizing something important, he said, "Actually, we will sail right past Martin and Île de Sein on our way home…" and his voice trailed off.

Bridgit noted silently that he said he would sail past Martin, but not his father.

She wondered at the omission but didn't say anything.

"I'll be back," Jack said suddenly as he straightened up and walked off, leaving Bridgit alone by the railing.

"Well, at least I know I am on a British ship headed for England," Bridgit thought to herself, still attempting to make sense of where she was and what was happening, "and I presume that will have to do for now." She let out an audible sigh.

Sometime later Jack returned with some rations and a cup of hot tea for each of them. Bridgit reflected this was yet one more time this man had come to her rescue.

"So, is that where you learned to speak French?" she asked after taking several sips of the sweet, piping hot nectar.

"From my mother, you mean?" Jack replied and Bridgit nodded, taking another mouthful of tea.

"Yes, I suppose so. It wasn't so much that I ever learned French. More that my mother seemed to float from one language to the other so often I became proficient through sheer necessity." He smiled at the memory.

"Did you ever see your brother and father again after you were separated?" she asked, now curious to know more.

"They came to Torquay one summer. I still have a photo of the four of us taken on Princess Pier. Martin and I must have been about fifteen, I think," he replied.

"You were *both* fifteen?" Bridgit asked quizzically.

Jack chuckled. "Yes – we're twins. Identical twins. I used to wonder if that's why our parents separated us – so they could tell us apart," he laughed. "It's like they always had one of us each. When we were born, my parents each decided to name one of us. My father named me after Jack Dempsey the boxer. He was a real man's man, my father and I took after him much more than my mother; and Martin is so much like our mother. She named him Martin after the French neurologist, Jean-Martin Charcot."

Bridgit's look was one of obviously needing more information.

"My mother always dreamed of being a scientist. She was fascinated by the impact that thought could have on a person's physiology and she wanted to study that," Jack continued. "Her favourite quote was by Charcot and I still remember her reciting it to me when I had certain ideas about something and wouldn't budge. She would parrot it off in whichever language she was using at the time." Putting on a high-pitched French accent to obviously parody his mother, he continued. "In the last analysis, we see only what we are ready to see, what we have been taught to see. We eliminate and ignore everything that is not a part of our prejudices" – and you are *obviously* not ready to see!" she would state with passion and conviction." Jack laughed to himself.

Bridgit thought back to her conversation with Markus. Charcot's quotation had a similar ring to it...

"...and I always thought it was funny that my English father moved to France, and my French mother stayed in England. I'm like my father but I stayed with our mother; and Martin is like our mother but stayed with our father. I'm from a crazy family," he smiled.

Bridgit cupped her hands around the still warm mug.

"So, what about you?" Jack asked. "Where is home for you?"

Bridgit wanted to say, "1895" but she bit her bottom lip to stop the words from tumbling out on their own.

"Warrior Square. Do you know it?" she asked, not sure what or how much to say.

Jack laughed out loud in a way that made several people near them smile simply from hearing the sound.

"The day we left to move to Torquay was the day after the Hastings Pier burned down back in July of 1917," he replied. "We must have been practically neighbours!"

Bridgit inaudibly remembered being a young child when, on an August Bank Holiday in 1872 the Earl of Granville officially opened the Hastings Pier on a day that was so blustery and rainy she was surprised anyone came out to witness the event.

Even the Brassy family who arrived for the event in their private steam ship, the 'Eothen', ricocheted so many times against the landing stage that some thought a disaster imminent.

Bridgit would meet Lady Brassey when Lord Brassey opened the St Leonard's Pier and years later would be thankful the Brasseys took her beloved and recently orphaned friend Elizabeth under their wing when the family moved to Australia.

Bridgit had regularly walked along Hastings Pier and now shuddered at the thought of the magnificent jetty going up in flames. In fact, she was headed to the

Pier the day she ran headlong into Dr Charles Preston... The memory now catching in her heart and throat.

Jack saw her contemplation and waited for Bridgit to continue, but when she didn't, he said, "they have a radio inside. What say we go in and see what's playing?"

It was now dark, and the two shivering souls made their way in to a crammed room where the BBC could be heard on the radio. Bridgit looked around for the source of the voice, but no-one appeared to be speaking.

At 19:00 GMT, a French voice came over the airwaves. It was the voice of Charles de Gaulle in a nationwide broadcast call for resistance to all French men and women.

It wasn't until someone said, "turn it up," and a man reached over, turned a knob, and the voice became louder did Bridgit then make the connection between the box and the sound.

"Who speaks French?" one soldier asked as others looked around.

Without pausing to reply, Jack began to translate de Gaulle's words…

"The leaders who, for many years, have been at the head of the French armies have formed a government. This government, alleging the defeat of our armies, has made contact with the enemy in order to stop the fighting. It is true, we were, we are, overwhelmed by the mechanical, ground and air forces of the enemy. Infinitely more than their number, it is the tanks, the aeroplanes, the tactics of the Germans which are causing us to retreat. It was the tanks, the aeroplanes, the tactics of the Germans that surprised our leaders to the point of bringing them to where they are today.

"But has the last word been said? Must hope disappear? Is defeat final? No! Believe me, I who am speaking to you with full knowledge of the facts, and who tell you that nothing is lost for France. The same means that overcame us can bring us victory one day. For France is not alone! She is not alone! She is not alone! She has a vast Empire behind her. She can align with the British Empire that holds the sea and continues the fight. She can, like England, use without limit the immense industry of the United States."

Bridgit observed the collective of men in the room. Some clearly interested, others staring blankly into nothingness...

"This war is not limited to the unfortunate territory of our country. This war is not over as a result of the Battle of France. This war is a world war. All the mistakes, all the delays, all the suffering, do not alter the fact that there are, in the world, all the means necessary to crush our enemies one day. Vanquished today by mechanical force, in the future we will be able to overcome by a superior mechanical force. The fate of the world depends on it."

"The fate of the world depends on it?" thought Bridgit with alarm. She had no idea that basically the whole world was at war.

"I, General de Gaulle, currently in London, invite the officers and the French soldiers who are located in British territory or who might end up here, with their weapons or without their weapons, I invite the engineers and the specialised workers of the armament industries who are located in British territory or who might end up here, to put themselves in contact with me.

"Whatever happens, the flame of the French resistance must not be extinguished and will not be extinguished. Tomorrow, as today, I will speak on the radio from London."

At the end of the broadcast, one soldier simply turned off the radio and the room fell silent.

What Jack didn't know what that on the tiny island of Île de Sein, his brother Martin was also listening to the broadcast along with the majority of the island's inhabitants.

Upon hearing the call to action, over three nights almost every man on the island between the ages of 15 and 54 boarded an array of small vessels bound for Penzance to join de Gaulle's Free French Force in England – Martin among them.

"Let's catch a kip," Jack said. "We'll find you a nice cosy spot to curl up. I'll head back up on deck."

Bridgit wasn't sure what he meant as the last she knew, a 'kip' meant a house of ill-repute, but she quickly discovered in this instance it meant to sleep.

Finding a small space in a corner, Bridgit was out before her head touched the rolled-up piece of cloth she was using as a pillow.

Chapter Four – "This Never Happened"

Awaking with a thudding headache and a churning stomach, Bridgit was disappointed to realize she was still aboard the ship, still covered in oil, and had not been transported to some other time and/or place while she slept. Slowly she managed to stand up, wrap her blanket again tightly around her shoulders and make her way topside.

With the majority of those on board still a greasy black mess, it was difficult to tell one person from another. She thought she recognized a man who had been on the same fishing boat but when he looked at her, she wasn't sure if that was him or not.

At over 320 feet in length, the Highlander was carrying back so many people to England, Bridgit felt a sudden sense of panic that she would not be able to find Jack – the only person she knew in this time and place.

Thinking she heard Jack's voice, Bridgit spun around and bumped into a man who was walking past her.

"Oh, excuse me," said Bridgit hurriedly stepping backward and almost tripping.

The man held out his hand to steady her. "It's quite all right," said the man who was about her age and, Bridgit was delighted to see, was not covered in oil – well, that is apart from where she had collided with him.

Bridgit smiled at him and the man responded with, "Frank Clements. Pleased to meet you."

Bridgit smiled. "My father's name was Frank." Then, learning from her meeting with Jack, Bridgit simply replied, "My name is Bridgit. Hello," and shook his hand.

Noticing something hanging from a thin strap that went around the man's shoulder and neck, Bridgit asked, "do you mind telling me, what is that?"

Frank Clements, with great pride and passion, removed the camera from around his neck and showed it to Bridgit.

"It's quite a spot of luck is what it is," said Clements. "I wasn't really supposed to have a camera but being a volunteer and since I didn't have any film, they didn't seem to mind – but then I bumped into a chap on my way to St Nazaire who had film and no camera! So, we did a trade for a new pair of socks from the NAAFI stores. I found myself with camera AND film."

He patted his beloved camera, "and in here are the last images of many a soul who didn't make it when that ship was sunk."

Clements would later go on to give the images of the sinking Lancastria and its aftermath to a man he met in a pub in England, who would then subsequently sell them to the press. What neither

Clements nor Bridgit knew was that those were the only photographs taken of an event that had been slapped with a wartime D-notice, meaning, as far as the rest of the world was concerned – it never happened.

Upon hearing of the disaster, Churchill immediately hid the news from the public.

The Dunkirk evacuation had only been a couple of weeks earlier and it was considered that to reveal the truth about the Lancastria would have been too damaging for civilian morale. Churchill said, 'The newspapers have got quite enough disaster for today, at least,' and imposed a media blackout. Furthermore, soldiers were told not to speak of the event to anyone or risk a court-martial.

So, for all intents and purposes, this – the greatest ever maritime disaster in British history and the largest single loss of life for British forces in the whole of World War II – never, ever happened.

Chapter Five - Plymouth

"There you are," Jack said and smiled as he walked toward Bridgit and Clement.

"Well, I'll be off. Good luck, Bridgit," Clement said as he continued on his way.

"I thought you might be up so I grabbed us some breakfast. They were all out of Eggs Benedict and caviar, but it's better than nothing," he joked as he offered some rations to Bridgit along with hot tea in a brown enamel mug.

The two found a place to sit and silently ate and drank their sustenance before Jack spoke again.

"What will happen to you when we get back to Plymouth?" he asked.

"Plymouth? Oh, is that where we are headed?" Bridgit asked in reply.

"Apparently so. I was speaking with some of the crew and they said we should arrive in a couple of hours." Jack took another mouthful of tea.

The futility of her situation again struck Bridgit. Of course, she knew where Plymouth was, but she had no idea how to get from there to St Leonard's/Hastings - and even if she did, she was obviously no longer in 1895! What would she find even if she could make her way back?

She began to tremble and as the colour drained from her face, Jack reached out and put his arm around her shoulders - and at this moment, she didn't care how improper the action. Bridgit merely accepted the gesture.

Minutes later and still not receiving a verbal response from Bridgit, Jack's mind raced for a way to fix the situation.

"Look, how about this," he finally said. "When we land, I will have to find my unit but before I go, I will make sure you have some money and supplies, and I'll get you to the train station and onto a train at least heading in the right direction, OK?" His look was almost pleading in the hope that this would be enough to make sure Bridgit was safe and that she would then feel secure enough to continue on her own.

Bridgit again nodded in agreement and in a quiet voice said, "thank you, Jack".

"You're very welcome – and thank you!" he replied.

"For what?" Bridgit asked, the colour beginning to return to her complexion.

"That's the first time you have said my name since we met," he replied and at that, Bridgit's cheeks blossomed into various shades of scarlet.

They both laughed a little as she put the back of her hand to her now very flushed cheek.

"Jack," she paused for effect and smiled, "may I ask you something?"

"Of course, m'lady," he replied in a playfully teasing tone.

"It's something you said about your mother." She looked at him but he didn't say anything so she continued.

"Do you – or did she – really believe that about our thoughts? That thought can affect more than just our mood – that it can actually affect us physically?" she continued.

Jack made himself a little more comfortable before responding. "Actually, I do," he replied. "There are so many things that are beyond our understanding and I believe that the power of our thoughts is one of them." He looked at her and said, "why do you ask?"

Bridgit was about to take him into her confidence but at the last instant decided not to. "Just curious," she replied, and with that the conversation moved on to the typically English subject – no matter what the century – of the weather, just as someone called out that Plymouth Harbour had come into view.

As the destroyer moored and people began disembarking, Jack said hurriedly to Bridgit, "if we get separated, meet me at the Mayflower Hotel at the Barbican. Just mention my name and they will take good care of you until I get there, OK?"

"All right," said Bridgit and did her best to put a brave smile on her face. "The Mayflower Hotel on Barbican," she repeated as she became lost in the crowd.

Thankfully, Jack's emergency plan was not needed. Bridgit was among the first women and children to disembark and since Jack positioned himself as close to the front of the men as possible, not far from the end of the gangway the two were reunited.

"OK, first things first," said Jack chirpily. "Let's see what we can do about getting cleaned up!"

Making their way from the dock, Jack and Bridgit passed person after person who were giving the survivors food, money, cigarettes, clothing...

The Salvation Army were distributing tea, sandwiches, fish and chips... They also had postcards for those who wanted to write home that they were safe... One man who had written a note to that effect and his home address on an empty cigarette packet pressed the paper into the hands of one of the Salvation Army members and implored the man, "send this, will you?"

As they continued, they even passed a young woman who was asking survivors to sign her autograph book.

Finally, they arrived at the Mayflower Hotel and upon walking through the door, Bridgit watched Jack disappear into the blackness that was a mixture of the cosy, dark interior, her eyes adjusting from being outside, and Jack's still black oil-covered, half-naked body.

"Hello, hello, hello! Anyone home?" Jack called to a man who was standing behind the bar.

"Jack? Is that you?" replied the bartender. "My God, man, what happened to you?" he continued as he also looked Bridgit up and down.

"Long story and I don't have much time, but do you think we could clean up a bit?" Jack asked.

"Of course, of course! Come this way," the portly yet fit-looking man in his fifties said as he showed Bridgit and Jack through to the back.

Providing them each with soap and water the man went to leave them to it then stopped and said, "just a minute, lassie."

He disappeared for a moment and came back with a small amount of sugar in a cup. "Works a treat for getting off grease. It's not enough to do all of you, but mix it with the soap and I thought it might help with your face and hair."

"You must be something special," smiled Jack noting the rationed gift his friend had bestowed upon Bridgit.

Having cleaned up as best they could, and Jack now wearing a shirt and shoes courtesy of one of the hotel's patrons, he and the bartender gave each other a hug, patted each other on the back and said their farewells.

Before leaving, the man pressed some money into Jack's hand.

"No, I couldn't," Jack protested.

"It's not for you, ya lump. It's for the lassie. Now be off with ya – and take care, ya hear?" The man gave a kindly smile, Jack nodded in reply, and with that Jack and Bridgit were again on their way, at least now a little cleaner and Jack a little less naked.

Unfortunately, less than twelve months later, the Mayflower Hotel was destroyed on March 21st, 1941 during the Blitz and along with it, their friendly bartender and fourteen others who were staying at the hotel.

Chapter Six – Hastings 45 Years Later…

The pair made their way to Plymouth Railway Station where literally thousands of people were cramming on to the various trains as they arrived.

In addition to the soldiers, the platforms were teeming with previous residents of the Channel Islands who, after June 15th when the British government decided that the Channel Islands were of no strategic importance and would not be defended, made the heart-wrenching decision to leave behind their possessions and flee to the mainland. Those who stayed found their home occupied by Nazi German forces on June 30th. Until they were liberated on May 9th, 1945, the Channel

Islands were the only British territories to be occupied by German forces during the entirety of the war.

Bridgit felt frozen to the spot as she watched the masses moving like a swarm of insects, only to be engulfed by the snake-like train.

"I don't know where I am or what I am doing here, but I want to go home," she thought despondently to herself.

Jack put his hand on Bridgit's arm and turned her to face him.

"OK, I want you to take this," he said as he put the money the bartender had given him into Bridgit's hand along with some of his own money. "It will be enough to see you through for a week or so. Maybe more."

Bridgit stared at the notes in her hand as she thought to herself that money had never really meant anything to her before now. Her father had always taken care of everything and even when he passed, Mrs Dixon took charge of the household accounts, "until you have a chance to get over the shock, Miss," Dixon said more than once - but Bridgit left before that ever happened...

"...and take this," Jack said as he reached into his pocket and pulled out a bent old coin. "It's Roman. Martin and I found it one day while we were on holiday. It may be a bit battered, but it's brought me plenty of luck so far," he placed it in

Bridgit's hand, "and I want you to have it."

Bridgit looked at the coin, turning it over several times but not saying a word.

"Tell me you will be OK," said Jack, sounding more like a question.

"I am sure I will be fine," replied Bridgit mustering as much courage as she could since she didn't really see any alternative at this moment.

"You really are something special," Jack chuckled as he gently wiped some still slightly oil-laden hair that had fallen in front of her face.

With that, Jack leaned toward Bridgit ever so slowly and kissed her delicately but passionately on the lips.

"Charles, I..." gasped Bridgit, the kiss having caught her completely off-guard.

"Well, that's one way to dent a chap's ego," said Jack as he took a step back.

"Oh, Jack. I am so sorry," said Bridgit, not sure how to remedy her error – and not sure why she made such an error in the first place.

"It's my fault. I didn't think you were involved with anyone – but then again, I didn't ask. I'm the one who is sorry."

With that, neither said another word and with military precision, Jack instantly took on the task of getting Bridgit on a train bound for Bristol – and Bridgit thought how much his pragmatism reminded her of beloved Dixon.

As she was about to board the carriage, Bridgit stopped and turned back to look at Jack.

"I will never forget you, Jack Dempsey," said Bridgit through tears and leaned over, kissing him lovingly on the cheek.

At that moment, the train began to inch forward and Jack became lost in a sea of faces…

A soldier gave up his seat for Bridgit who almost instantly became lost in thought.

"Why did I mention Charles' name?" she mulled over in her mind, "and why do I feel as though I owe him an apology?"

The more Bridgit thought, the more confused she became so she decided to focus on the task at hand – getting back to Hastings, or more specifically, back to Warrior Square in St Leonards On Sea.

She wasn't sure why since the likelihood of anyone in this time knowing her was essentially naught – and even her home was most likely now owned by someone else... That thought caught her heart in a way she hadn't expected.

"I never thought of that... I mean, if my home isn't even my home anymore..." she started questioning herself and just as she began entering a whirl of dire possibilities in her head, the train pulled in to Bristol station.

Bridgit then thankfully needed to focus on making her way piecemeal half-way across England, sleeping overnight on one platform, to finally arrive at St Leonard's Station.

Stepping on to the platform, Bridgit let out a sigh of relief.

"At least this place still looks basically the same," she said aloud.

Noticing a newspaper on the ground, Bridgit bent down, picked it up and looked at the masthead.

"It is even the same newspaper," she smiled to herself – until she read the date: 20th June, 1940.

"1940?!" Alarms went off in her head. "I knew I had travelled forward in time, but 45 years?"

Closing her eyes momentarily and taking a deep breath, Bridgit then opened her eyes wide, took another deep breath, put the newspaper back down and decided to press on.

Searching for a sense of optimism from familiar surroundings, Bridgit climbed the stairs, walked over the footbridge, down the other side and made her way down the hill toward Warrior Square.

Bridgit was amazed that, apart from the vehicles and the clothes worn by the people she saw, nothing seemed to have changed – nothing at all!

Upon reaching what had been her house on the westerly side of the Square, Bridgit stopped at the bottom of the stairs.

A young couple in their early twenties came out of the door. "Can we help you?" they asked.

Realizing that her home was no longer her home, Bridgit said, "no, I must have the wrong house. Thank you," and proceeded toward the shore.

Here, she finally saw what had changed.

No longer the peaceful, beautiful seaside vista of the English Channel, now what greeted her was barbed wire fencing and large criss-crossed barricades.

"If everything else is at least intact, perhaps the Royal Victoria Hotel will still be a hotel," she thought to herself and turned right at the bottom of the Square.

Sure enough, the Royal Victoria Hotel was still standing and was still a hotel.

Bridgit booked herself into one of the rooms and, when the attendant asked if she had any luggage – and looked rather surprisedly at her still oil stained body and clothing – Bridgit suddenly became self-conscious of her appearance.

"Actually, no," she replied as she attempted to smooth her hair and straighten her clothing.

"Just wait here a moment please," said the attendant. Minutes later an older, stout woman walked over to Bridgit.

"Will you please come with me?" the woman asked in an authoritarian yet caring tone.

Dutifully following, Bridgit was shown into a side room where the woman smiled at her and said, "so tell me. How did you end up like this?"

What Bridgit didn't realize was that before the woman offered any assistance, she was doing her best to ascertain whether Bridgit was indeed a German spy.

The attendant was alerted not only because of her appearance and lack of luggage but, as he said to the woman, "her English is just a little too good!"

Convinced of Bridgit's story about being onboard a shipwreck, the woman assured the attendant that Bridgit should be given a room, sent out for some clothes to be procured, walked Bridgit up to her accommodation and even began the process of running her a hot bath before wishing her luck and returning downstairs.

Now safely in a room that had a bed and thankfully a bath, Bridgit for the first time since she 'arrived' in this time and place saw herself in a mirror and let out an audible gasp of shock.

Letting out a sigh that dropped her shoulders several inches, Bridgit began to undress to take her bath and was amazed at the lack of underclothes she was wearing. Only a type of small corset that covered her breasts but nothing below them, a satin chemise, and underpants.

Finally stepping into the comfort and reassuring feeling of hot, clean water, Bridgit settled herself, her head propped on the end of the tub, and within minutes fell asleep.

Mercifully waking before the water had gone completely cold, Bridgit subsequently did her best to remove all traces of the disaster from her outer being, although much of it ended up on the towel as she dried herself off.

Dressing in the clothes the woman had provided, Bridgit at least felt slightly more human than she had done on her arrival, and feeling the sudden onset of ravenous hunger, proceeded to the dining room for some sustenance.

She was immediately seated next to a large window and as she was looking out across the English Channel, Bridgit became aware of an elderly man at the next table who seemed to be staring at her.

Taking the initiative, Bridgit looked at him and asked, "may I help you, sir?"

"Why, yes, if you don't mind," said the man as he rose from his seat and stood beside Bridgit's table. Motioning to the empty chair he said, "do you mind?"

Reflecting that she had experienced far greater affronts to what she would call 'normal' behaviour over the past couple of days, she replied, "please do."

The man was tall, very well-dressed, approximately seventy years of age and had an elegant manner and bearing.

"Excuse me for intruding," he began, "but I couldn't help but notice your necklace." Bridgit instinctively reached for the piece hanging around her neck. "Did your mother or grandmother perhaps give that to you?"

Thinking back to the day Elizabeth had given her the cross – one of two identical crosses Elizabeth's father had made for his wife and daughter - Bridgit smiled sadly at the memory.

"No. It was given to me by a dear friend," she replied.

"Then perhaps it was your friend's mother or grandmother who gave it to them?" His question seemed odd and rather intrusive.

Feeling more than a little miffed, Bridgit responded in a bristling tone. "No, as I said, a very dear friend of mine gave me the necklace when she left to go to Australia." The man's eyes became wide and his face slightly pale - an expression Bridgit mistook as disbelief so she continued. "If you must know, it is one of two identical crosses and my friend has the other one."

"Had," said the man.

"Excuse me," replied Bridgit, not sure what he meant.

"Elizabeth HAD the other one," as he took from his coat pocket a small gold cross on a dainty gold chain and laid it carefully on the table.

Bridgit stared at the cross. It was identical to the one that hung around her neck.

...and then it struck her – he had mentioned Elizabeth. Bridgit was sure she had not said her name aloud.

Neither person spoke. Bridgit gently removed the cross from around her neck and laid it beside the one on the table. They were identical.

Silence hung over them like a winter blanket until the man began to speak...

"What I don't understand," he said, "is why you said Elizabeth gave this to *you*?" He paused, "surely you mean she gave it to your mother?" Not getting any response except a confused expression on Bridgit's face, he continued. "I mean, you look almost identical to your ancestor, Lady Bridgit Darnell, Elizabeth's friend. My wife had a photo of her friend that she kept along with photos of her parents. But it was about fifty years ago that Elizabeth left England for Australia, so surely you must mean she gave the cross to your mother?"

There was too much information in the man's speech to process all at once and Bridgit just sat there, dumbfounded – literally.

"You look pale. Let me get you some water," said the man and attracted the attention of a waiter who quickly fetched a glass of water for Bridgit.

As she was replaying and processing everything in her mind, one phrase stood out – 'my wife' – and Bridgit stopped.

"Your *wife*?" she asked the man incredulously.

"Yes," replied the man, a little confused by the tone of the question. "Elizabeth Bartlett was my wife."

...and then another word that felt out of place – 'was'.

"What do you mean, *was*, exactly?" asked Bridgit, although she felt in her heart she knew the answer.

"My wife passed away a little over two years ago," he added with genuine love and still more than a little anguish.

Bridgit took a deep breath – and another – and another... She felt as though the walls were curving in on top of her and the lights were being dimmed.

Just before she felt she was about to pass out, Bridgit stood up and said, "I need some air," as she headed down to and out of the front door of the hotel.

She crossed the road and stood holding on to the barbed-wire topped fence that now separated the beach from the rest of Hastings/St Leonards.

Doing her best to slow her breathing, taking in the fresh, salty air, Bridgit began processing what she had heard.

Elizabeth was dead. Of course, this 'now' was actually forty-five years after she left so it stood to reason, but it was still hard to imagine.

...and this man in the hotel had been Elizabeth's husband.

As she thought of Elizabeth, Bridgit reached for her necklace and, finding her neck bare, realized she had left the cross on the table in the hotel.

Although part of her wanted to quickly head back in to retrieve the beloved item, another part of her wanted to tear open the fence, walk into the water and just swim into oblivion.

Then, she thought of Jack... "I wonder where he is," she pondered.

Bridgit reflected back to the kiss on the platform and still kicked herself for saying Charles' name... "Charles... Where are you?" she thought aloud and then realized that, just like Elizabeth, Charles, too, was most likely already dead.

Bridgit was numb, but having no other alternative than to continue this journey she had begun by means of her 'dream' conversation with Markus, she let go of the fence, straightened her hair, stood tall and walked, refined and erect, back to the hotel and up to the dining room where the man was still sitting at the table.

Chapter Seven ~ Revelation

Seating herself at the table, noting the two necklaces still lying side by side, Bridgit looked at the man and asked, "sir, may I ask you a question?"

"Of course," he replied and gave Bridgit a polite smile.

"When did you and Elizabeth marry?"

His smile broadened as he thought about his beloved. "It was the first of August, 1897 – and I remember it as if it was yesterday..." The man's voice trailed off as he delved into his memories.

"...and was she happy?" asked Bridgit.

Blinking to come back to this moment, the man looked at Bridgit with contemplation, not sure what to make of the questions she was asking.

"Yes, very," he replied. "The Brasseys were very good to her – and then she and I had a wonderful life," he again smiled. "Well, of course, every couple has their ups and downs, but she was my everything." His eyes glistened with love.

Realizing she had little other options, and sensing a safe place to share her story, Bridgit still took another moment or two to decide whether to divulge her fantastical account, before speaking...

"Sir, I have... I'm sorry, I don't even know your name," Bridgit apologized to the man.

"Bartlett. Franklin Bartlett," he replied.

"Another Frank," Bridgit mused silently to herself and inwardly sent her father a kiss.

"Mr Bartlett," she began. "I would like to tell you how I came by that necklace and then how I arrived here," she said, motioning to the hotel itself, "but I need for you not to say a word until I have finished. Is that all right with you?"

The man tipped his head on the side, not sure what to make of this, but said, "I suppose so," and nodded, prompting Bridgit to commence her statement.

Bridgit began at the beginning, with the dream about Markus, and included everything from her father's death to Charles' betrayal – but when she reached the part of Elizabeth's parents passing away and the young girl leaving for Australia, Mr Bartlett held up his hand to stop her.

"I'm sorry, but you must be mistaken. There is no way you could have known this unless someone told you." He now seemed hurt and irate as he continued. "You must be all of thirty," he said.

"Thirty-one," interjected Bridgit, and then said, "please, will you just let me continue and then I will answer any question you might have – or I will get up and walk away if that is what you wish – but please, just allow me to finish…" she pleaded with him. Now that she had started sharing this incredible journey,

Bridgit felt she couldn't stop, no matter what.

Mr Bartlett remained silent and with a cross look on his face, nodded his compliance for Bridgit to continue.

She took a deep breath and picked up where she left off – the moment Elizabeth gave her the necklace... finally ending with how she came to be sitting here at the table.

The man wasn't merely staring at Bridgit. It was as though he was scanning every minute detail of her face, looking for any anomaly that would prove her to be lying.

Eventually he reached down, picked up one of the necklaces and said, "I need time to process this. Meet me here tomorrow at five in the afternoon," and without getting a response from Bridgit, he walked sternly away.

The next twenty-four hours felt to Bridgit as though they were one-hundred hours or more while she waited for five o'clock to come around.

Punctually at the stroke of five, Mr Bartlett walked into the dining room and over to the table at which Bridgit sat.

"All right, young lady," he began. "I am prepared to hear you out, but I have a few questions of my own."

Bridgit sat even straighter in her chair and prepared for her inquisition, determined not to keep anything back.

Mr Bartlett barraged Bridgit with question after question about Elizabeth's history, doing all he could to find something, anything, that would shoot a hole in Bridgit's story, but eventually his interrogation ran out of steam and he sat back in his chair and let out an audible sigh…

"Well, then," he began anew. "It seems I may have misjudged you," he paused, "and also that you have found yourself in one fine pickle, Lady Bridgit!"

This was the first time anyone had called her *Lady* Bridgit since her adventure began. There was something safe and comforting in the address.

"So, you believe me?" asked Bridgit.

"It is a fanciful tale," he replied, "but I can see nor sense any deceit nor inconsistencies in your account so yes, I am inclined to believe you, my dear."

Bridgit wanted to cry but held in her tears.

"Now, if I am not mistaken," he continued, "the next thing we need to do is to work out how to get you home."

Home! That word had never rung so true and clear. That's what Bridgit wanted – to find 'home' – and she realized at that moment, home may not appear to be what it did, but it was how she felt.

Home was being surrounded by people she knew and loved who knew and loved her. It wasn't about a particular house on a particular street – and it wasn't even about a particular moment in time.

Bridgit thought about her father and while she deeply longed to be reunited with him, there was an ever-present thought that she would at some point have to go through the process of losing him all over again, and she didn't feel she had the strength to do that. Once was enough.

"What if I stay here?" Bridgit addressed her question out the window before turning back to face Mr Bartlett.

"You mean, not travel to another time or another place?" he asked, "but stay here where you don't know anyone?"

"Yes." Bridgit stopped to fully consider what she was saying. "What if I make here and now my home?"

She looked back out the window before continuing. "I know you now," she smiled and he returned the gesture, "so that's a good start."

The two chuckled and he replied, "actually, if you weren't technically older than me, I would almost look at you like a daughter," he grinned in reply.

Bridgit laughed out loud. It felt good to laugh.

Laughter. That is another element of 'home', she thought.

"I know Jack, even though I don't know where he is," Bridgit continued, now feeling her rationale growing stronger.

"All right," said Mr Bartlett. "Let's say you do make 'now' your home, we will need to make some preparations for you, starting with a place to live. As lovely as it is, you cannot live in a hotel for the rest of your life." Bridgit smiled.

"What's say I make some enquiries tomorrow and we again meet back here at five," he said as he stood up.

Bridgit nodded, too emotional to speak.

That night, Bridgit was lying in bed thinking about the events she had experienced since landing here in 1940. Mostly she thought about Jack.

Reaching over to the table beside the bed, Bridgit picked up the 'lucky' coin Jack had given to her.

Clutching it in her hand, she whispered, "wherever you are, Jack, be safe," and with that she drifted off to sleep.

Chapter Eight ~ What is 'Now'?

As Bridgit awoke, she was surprised to realize the sun was not shining in through the casements.

When she arose to investigate, she discovered heavy black curtains pulled across the windows.

"That's funny," she thought to herself as she opened them, allowing the sun to stream into the room. "I don't remember those being here last night."

Bridgit dressed and decided to go for a walk on such a lovely-looking day.

Even as she walked through the reception area, though, Bridgit felt something was different.

Not sure what it was, or even if it was just her imagination, Bridgit continued out the front door of the hotel and turned left along seafront, toward Warrior Square.

Almost immediately, Bridgit felt a sinking feeling begin in her stomach - a feeling that deepened and intensified the further she walked.

One moment buildings were intact, the next there was a hole where she was certain yesterday there was a house.

When she reached Warrior Square, although most of the Square was intact, there was a gaping hole where once there were majestic houses.

Feeling totally disoriented, Bridgit continued along the shore toward Hastings Old Town and came across a statue of Queen Victoria – the queen to whom Bridgit had been a loyal subject.

As she passed, Bridgit noticed a hole in the statue, right through Queen Victoria's skirt.

"Odd," mused Bridgit, but didn't give it another thought as she continued.

Three soldiers were walking toward her and one looked strangely familiar.

As they grew closer, Bridgit squinted as if to focus more intently, before realizing the soldier in the middle was Jack.

"Jack!" she exclaimed with joy and walked hurriedly toward the men.

The soldiers looked back and forth between each other before one patted the man in the middle on the shoulder and the other two continued passing Bridgit on either side, leaving her with the man she had just referred to as 'Jack'.

He stood looking her and while at first glance he appeared to be the Jack she knew, the more she studied his features and particularly his eyes, the more she was now confused.

"You knew Jack?" asked the man in a French accent.

Taken aback at hearing Jack's voice come out of a body that looked just like Jack – but wasn't... Bridgit simply replied, "yes."

"He was my brother," continued the man – and there it was again... The wrong tense as far as Bridgit was concerned.

'Elizabeth *was* my wife' and now 'Jack *was* my brother'.

Bridgit felt faint and the man she had thought was Jack steadied her and assisted her to a bench seat a little way further along the street.

Bridgit could not help but stare at this man who looked just like Jack.

"I know," he said, realizing her confusion. "We were identical twins. Even our parents could often not tell us apart." He smiled at her but all she could do was look at him in disbelief.

Feeling as though he had to fill the silence, the man continued. "I am Martin," he said and held out his hand. Bridgit limply offered hers and instead of shaking her hand, he kissed it.

She was caught off-guard, shocked and immediately withdrew her hand from his.

"I am sorry but you just looked so forlorn," Martin commented with an apologetic tone.

Bridgit's face was flushed and tears were welled up in her eyes.

"He was killed in the Loire Estuary," continued Martin, not sure whether to tell her or not but feeling as though she deserved to hear the truth. "The troopship he was on that was bringing him back to England was sunk and he was shot by a German plane while he was still in the water," he said.

"That can't be," exclaimed Bridgit, now standing and staring at Martin. "He didn't die in the water. I know he didn't. That's a mistake. He made it to shore. So that must mean he's alive!"

Bridgit smiled at Martin who didn't share her enthusiasm. She again looked puzzled as he reached for something in his pocket.

"I am sorry to tell you this, but he did die just off St Nazaire. His body was washed ashore and when his belongs were returned to me, this was among them."

Martin opened his palm and revealed Jack's lucky coin – the same lucky coin Bridgit had put on the table beside her bed last night.

"Are you ok?" he asked as all the colour drained from Bridgit's face.

All the elements of the day now coalesced into a cohesive picture – one that confirmed to Bridgit she had again travelled in time. Yesterday was obviously not 'yesterday' to Martin – and somehow in this 'today' Jack was dead but in her 'yesterday' he was still alive and well…

"Will you please walk me back to the hotel?" asked Bridgit. Martin offered her his arm to steady her and as they walked back to the Royal Victoria Hotel, Bridgit still had trouble separating that this man walking beside her was not Jack – and that in this reality, Jack was dead.

Seeing her safely back to her accommodation, Martin wished her well and went off to find his colleagues, leaving Bridgit to go back to her room alone.

As she opened the door, she ruminated the good fortune that at least she still had a room – but Jack was dead – and obviously more time had passed since she went to sleep.

She also thought about Markus' comment regarding what he called the 'grandfather paradox' that states you can't go back and kill your ancestor or you wouldn't be born. According to Markus' theory, when you travel back in time – "or perhaps forward," she thought – the ancestor doesn't die in that reality, but rather in a parallel one.

"So, Jack may be dead in *this* reality," she considered, "but in another reality he is still alive and safe." That thought comforted her somewhat.

Bringing her thoughts back to her now, Bridgit looked about the room. "What is the time?" she asked herself aloud, and then realized she didn't mean the hour on the clock – she mean the year on the calendar.

As Bridgit headed back down to reception to get an answer to her question, she thought about Mr Bartlett. Would he still be here? Was he still alive?

Upon reaching the front desk, she decided to answer those questions first.

"Excuse me," she asked the man behind the counter. "Is there a Mr Bartlett registered at the hotel?"

The clerk looked at his registration book and said, "No, I'm sorry miss. There is no one of that name currently registered here."

"Thank you," she said dejectedly and began walking away until the clerk called her back. "What would your name be if you don't mind me asking?" he said.

"Lady Bridgit Darnell," Bridgit replied, not sure why the clerk would ask.

"Then, Lady Darnell, yes. Mr Bartlett left a package for you in our safe. Just a moment while I go and get it."

Around five minutes passed and the clerk returned to the desk, handing an envelope to Bridgit. She thanked him and went back up to her room to open the package.

Sitting on her bed, Bridgit slowly opened the envelope and in it was Elizabeth's necklace and a note.

Dear Lady Bridgit,

When you did not show up to our meeting I wondered if you had been delayed. But when you did not appear for several weeks, I surmised that perhaps you had again 'travelled'.

I am leaving this afternoon to go back to Australia, but have notified my lawyers that in the event of my death, wherever and whenever that may be, Elizabeth's cross and an allowance that will ensure you are always provided for are to be delivered to the Royal Victoria Hotel and kept in their safe in case you ever return.

Take care, dear Bridgit, and if ever you see Elizabeth again, give her a kiss from me.

Warmest regards,
Franklin Bartlett.

Bridgit curled up on the bed and sobbed... Heart-wrenching, gut-wrenching sobs... until she finally cried herself to sleep.

Waking in the early evening, it took Bridgit a moment to again realize where – and when – she was, before she splashed cold water on her now puffy face and headed downstairs.

There was a collection of people in the lobby but the entire place was silent – except for a radio playing in the corner to which the entire group were fixated.

A man's voice came over the airwaves...

"Well that is of course what happens to us," the broadcast continued. "Our life comes to us moment by moment. One moment disappears before the next comes along: and there is room for very little in each. That is what Time is like."

The broadcaster was C. S. Lewis – the author who at this moment had already started writing, but not yet published, the 'Narnia' series – and on this twenty-ninth day of February, 1944 Bridgit was listening to the latest in his radio series that would eventually be published collectively as 'Mere Christianity'.

"And of course," he continued, "you and I tend to take it for granted that this Time series -- this arrangement of past, present and future -- is not simply the way life comes to us but the way all things really exist. We tend to assume that the whole universe and God Himself are always moving on from past to future just as we do. But many learned men do not agree with that. It was the Theologians who first started the idea that some things are not in Time at all: later the philosophers took it over: and now some of the scientists are doing the same."

Someone started talking and was shushed by the crowd.

"Almost certainly God is not in Time. His life does not consist of moments following one another. If a million people are praying to him at 10:30 tonight, he need not listen to them in that one little snippet which we call 10:30. 10:30 -- and every other moment from the beginning of the world -- is always the Present for Him. If you like to put it that way, he has all eternity in which to listen to the split second of prayer put up by a pilot as his plane crashes in flames.

"That is difficult I know. Let me try to give something, not the same, but a bit like it. Suppose I am writing a novel. I write "Mary laid down her work; next moment came a knock at the door!" For Mary who has to live in the imaginary time of my story there is no interval between putting down the work and hearing the knock. But I, who am Mary's maker, do not live in that imaginary time at all. Between writing the first half of that sentence and the second, I might sit down for three hours and think steadily about Mary. I could think about Mary as if she were the only character in the book and for as long as I pleased and the hours I spent in doing so would not appear in Mary's time (the time inside the story) at all.

"This is not a perfect illustration, of course. But it may give just a glimpse of what I believe to be the truth."

Bridgit left the group to continue listening to the radio and went back up to her room. "This is all just too much to consider at one moment," she thought to herself as she again sat back down on the bed.

Bridgit again felt totally lost. Everyone she knew and loved was dead, in some reality or other – and even though she knew by now in this time that Charles would almost certainly be dead as well, at least no one had told her as much.

"If I can't go home, I at least want to go back to my own time," Bridgit said aloud as she looked around her room at furniture and décor that bore no resemblance to the Victorian elegance she had known.

Eventually as she curled up to again go to sleep, Bridgit thought about Charles' letter and the posy ring he had given her.

The last thought she remembered as she drifted off to sleep was that she wished she had the ring with her now…

...and then...

"Are y'all right, miss?" Bridgit heard a deep male voice ask in a slow drawl.

As she opened her eyes, Bridgit saw a woman beside her fussing about, waving a handkerchief in Bridgit's face, and a tall figure of a man that seemed so large and impressive as to obliterate the entire view.

"She fainted when she heard about General Lee's surrender," said the woman in a high-pitched drawl that sounded to Bridgit as though the woman was doing her best to add the letter Y in the middle of as many words as possible. To Bridgit's ears it sounded like, "She faYinted when she heaYrd about General LeeYs surreYnder."

Bridgit had awoken in April, 1865 back in Charleston, South Carolina and at the end of a conflict that divided a nation – not just across the line delineating North and South, but across questions and arguments that still to this day have not been effectively answered, nor the wounds healed…

Over the coming days, Bridgit is witness to actions driven by both the highest ideals for which a man can stand and the lowest to which he can stoop – and she will completely reassess her definition and understanding of the entire concept of "**FREEDOM**" (and it will not be as 'black and white' as you might think…)

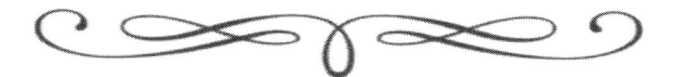

To stay up to date with the release of future books in the Quantum Lace series, please visit the website and add your email address to the notification list:

www.QuantumLace.com

...and I would really appreciate it if you would **leave a review on Amazon!** I look forward to hearing what you think...

Acknowledgements

It is always a tricky endeavour to thank people because there is always the tendency to forget someone!

So, first of all, anyone I haven't mentioned below – **thank you!** :-)

I would like to acknowledge and thank (not in any particular order):

- Victims and survivors of the sinking of HMT Lancastria, as well as those who participated in their rescue – and those who keep their memory alive.

- To the brave men of Île de Sein and others like them.

- To all who served in WWII and to those who didn't serve in the armed forces but whose sacrifices at home made the difference that made all the difference.

- Amanda Holden, her Uncle George Holden, and the entire "Who Do You Think You Are?" team for bringing the Lancastria to my attention in the first place – like many, I had never even heard of the disaster until I saw your program.

- Jonathan Fenby, Author of "The Sinking of the Lancastria" – your record of the tragedy is a remarkable capturing of an historical event.

- Jeremy Clarkson's "War Stories" that gave such a vivid picture of events in WWII (PS – please do more of them!)

- Lord Julian Fellowes who continues to provide inspiration and is my constant benchmark of true quality.

- Neil Oliver and the Team at "Coast" for your episode where I learned of the men of Île de Sein (and for all your episodes – I love the show!)

- The Giammei Family and their lovely penthouse apartment in Italy that I leased while completing this book.

- All the quantum physicists, historians, authors, presenters, researchers, seekers and others who have provided (and continue to provide in many cases) me with insights, knowledge and inspiration…

- …and everyone who loves to read and write books… You are the ones who keep Bridgit alive…

Thank you...

...and remember, if you would like me to email you when the next book is published, simply go to www.QuantumLace.com and provide me with your email address.

Well, now that Book Two is complete, it is time to curl up and dive into the research for Bridgit's next book.

Until then, sending love and smiles to all...

Bella St John

For more information on the series and contact details for the author, please visit:

www.QuantumLace.com

About the Author

Living a globe-trotting lifestyle that most people only dream about, Leigh (Bella) St John travels the world with several suitcases that her luggage concierge service picks up and delivers to her next exotic location – this book, for instance, was written in Vienna and Lido di Ostia in Italy.

The Quantum Lace series is a combination of many of Bella's personal loves – quantum physics; the Victorian Era; history in general and forgotten or little-known history in particular; and the quests and challenges – and more specifically how we view and handle them – that make us who we are...

If you look at Bella's 'Bucket List' (http://luxuriousnomad.com/bucket-list) you will see not only what she still wants to achieve, but also the incredible things she has already accomplished.

When you meet her, you instantly understand the meaning of the word "passion" – she lives & breathes it with an enthusiasm that is contagious!

For more information and/or to contact the author, please visit:

www.BellaStJohn.com

Printed in Poland
by Amazon Fulfillment
Poland Sp. z o.o., Wrocław